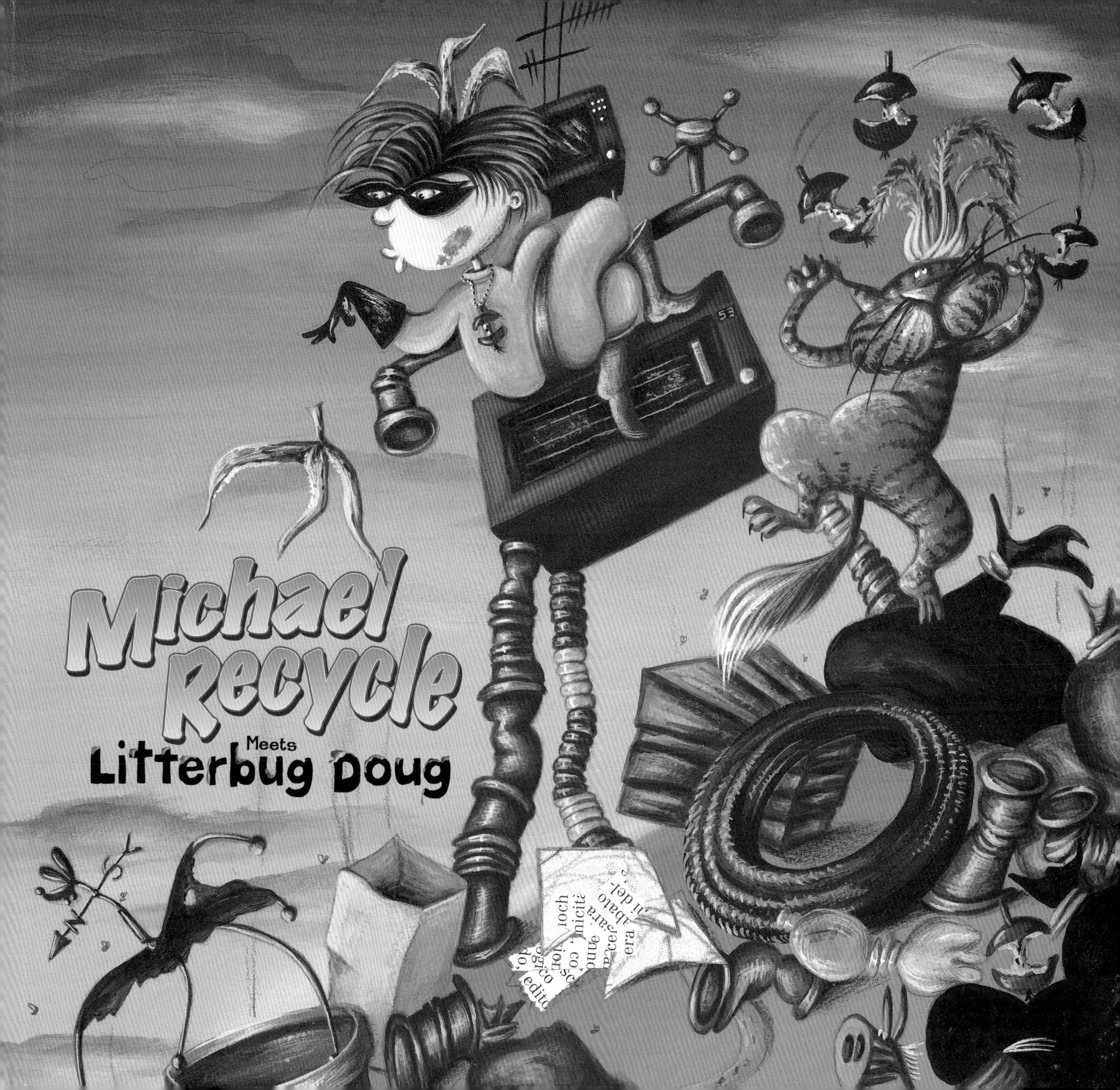
Michael Recycle
Meets
Litterbug Doug

www.MyWorthwhileBooks.com

ISBN: 978-1-60010-392-6

23 22 21 20   3 4 5 6

Litterbug Doug's trash facts are based on information from the U.S. Environmental Protection Agency. Visit www.epa.gov to find out even more information!

PRESENT:

WORTHWHILE
B O O K S

Published by arrangement with Meadowside Children's Books, 185 Fleet Street, London EC4A 2HS.

Worthwhile Books, a division of Idea and Design Works, LLC.
Editorial offices: 2765 Truxtun Road, San Diego, CA 92106. Printed in China.

Worthwhile Books does not read or accept unsolicited submissions of ideas, stories, or artwork.

Jonas Publishing, Publisher: Howard Jonas
IDW, Chairman: Morris Berger • IDW, President: Ted Adams • IDW, Senior Graphic Artist: Robbie Robbins
Worthwhile Books, Vice-President and Creative Director: Rob Kurtz • Worthwhile Books, Senior Editor: Megan Bryant

Michael Recycle
Meets Litterbug Doug

Written by
Ellie Bethel

Illustrated by
Alexandra Colombo

To my super-siblings,
Andrew and Jacqui . . .
thanks for all your
super-support!—E.B.

For Mummy, Gnome,
Pepi, Kay, and Enrico,
who help me every day
to become a better per-
son.—A.C.

In a beautiful valley
in the shade of a hill
was a clean little town
that was full of goodwill.

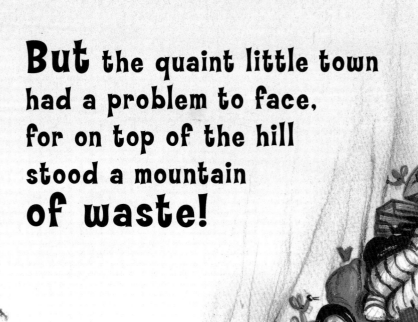

But the quaint little town
had a problem to face,
for on top of the hill
stood a mountain
of waste!

And who was
the culprit?
Who was the **thug?**
It was **lonely** and
lazy-boned . . .

Litterbug Doug!

His house was a garbage dump
full of old stuff
that was rotting and moldy
and smelly enough
to make your eyes water,
the stink was so strong;
but Doug didn't think he'd
done anything wrong.

And his only real friends
were a hundred-odd rats
(except for two lounging
and fat tabby cats).

From alone on his throne
Doug thoughtlessly threw
all manner of litter
and so the pile grew. . . .

A rotting banana,
some moldy old cheese.
Faulty fridge freezers
and smashed-up TVs!
Chewed-up old candy
that was no longer sweet—
all kinds of Doug's clutter
was hurled on the heap.

And then to the joy
of the hundred odd rats,
Doug even got rid of
his two tabby cats!

The cats were so plump
that they made the dump fall . . .

But then something happened
that none could explain.
It wasn't a bird and it wasn't a plane.

A green-caped crusader
stupendously swooped,
descending to Earth
with a great loop-the-loop!

"**Litterbug Doug**,"
said our green-hero,
Michael.

But Doug just retorted,
"I **won't** make amends. I **don't** need this town.
The rats are my friends!"

"But Doug, don't you care
that the litter you've hurled
is rotting and reeking,
polluting our world?

"It's hard to believe,
but I guess it depends;
do you really want rats
and not people as friends?"

Then thinking aloud, Doug said,
"I suppose. . . .

"They do give me fleas,
and they **nibble my toes!**
They make such a racket;
their hygiene's not great. . . .

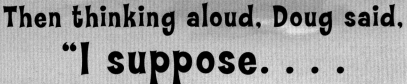

"I'd love some real friends,
but is it too late?"

"Of course not!" said Michael.

"All hands on the deck.
If we work hard together,
we can save you
just yet!"

They formed a big chain
from Doug's dump to Michael
(to sort out what's garbage and what to recycle).

And soon all the town
was so neat and pristine,
the only thing left was . . .

to give Doug
a clean!

And now he was neater
and no longer smelled,
so they gave him a job
at which Doug excelled.

Now watch out!
Don't litter
or drop one
small piece.

He's there in a flash. . . .

. . . Doug's the **litter police!**

Litterbug Doug's
Trash Roundup

TRASH TALK!

In 2007, Americans threw away almost 5 pounds of trash per person *per day*—that's more than 1,600 pounds of trash in a year for every man, woman, and child! That's half a hippo!

RECYCLING TO THE RESCUE!

Americans recycled 33 percent of the trash they threw away in 2007. (Another third was thrown away, and the rest is on the floor of your closet.)

PILE IT UP

Americans composted 22 million tons of materials in 2007. You can compost, too-just start a compost pile in your backyard! Mix grass clippings, fallen leaves, plant waste, vegetable and fruit peels, coffee grounds, and even eggshells in a pile in your yard. Even leftover broccoli and spinach can be composted! But don't add meat or dairy products to your compost pile. Once a week, stir the compost. A little sun, a little rain, a few bugs, and a few months will turn yard waste into healthy soil for your garden—instead of take up space in a land-fill.

WASTE NOT, WANT NOT

More than 85 million tons of waste were recycled or composted in 2007. When that number reaches 100 million tons, maybe the president will give everyone a free cheese-

CAN IT!

More than 60 percent of steel cans (and almost 50 percent of aluminum cans) are recycled every year. Don't throw that can in the trash—toss it in the recycling bin instead!

BLACK AND WHITE AND RECYCLED ALL OVER!

More than 50 percent of paper products were recycled in 2007. Help that number go up by recycling paper bags, computer paper, notebooks, cardboard boxes, newspapers, magazines, and catalogs! You can even recycle parking tickets and bad report cards!

DUMP THE LANDFILLS

There are more than 1,700 landfills in the United States. There were almost 8,000 just twenty years ago!

KEEP IT CLEAN

Recycling doesn't just save room in landfills. It also helps keep the air, water, and earth cleaner, too! Besides, it's cool to recycle.

Michael Recycle's Go Green Tips

RECYCLE EVERY DAY!

Recycle, recycle, recycle! Find out what can be recycled in your town—most towns offer curbside pickup of newspapers, cans, glass, and certain kinds of plastic. But you might also be able to recycle Styrofoam, aluminum foil, cardboard, catalogs and magazines, and even appliances and electronic equipment!

FLIP THE SWITCH

Save energy by turning off lights and electronic equipment when you leave the room.

TREES, PLEASE

Plant a tree! Trees help keep the earth cool and the air clean.

WATER WATCH

Save water by taking shorter showers (less than five minutes) and turning off the water while you brush your teeth.

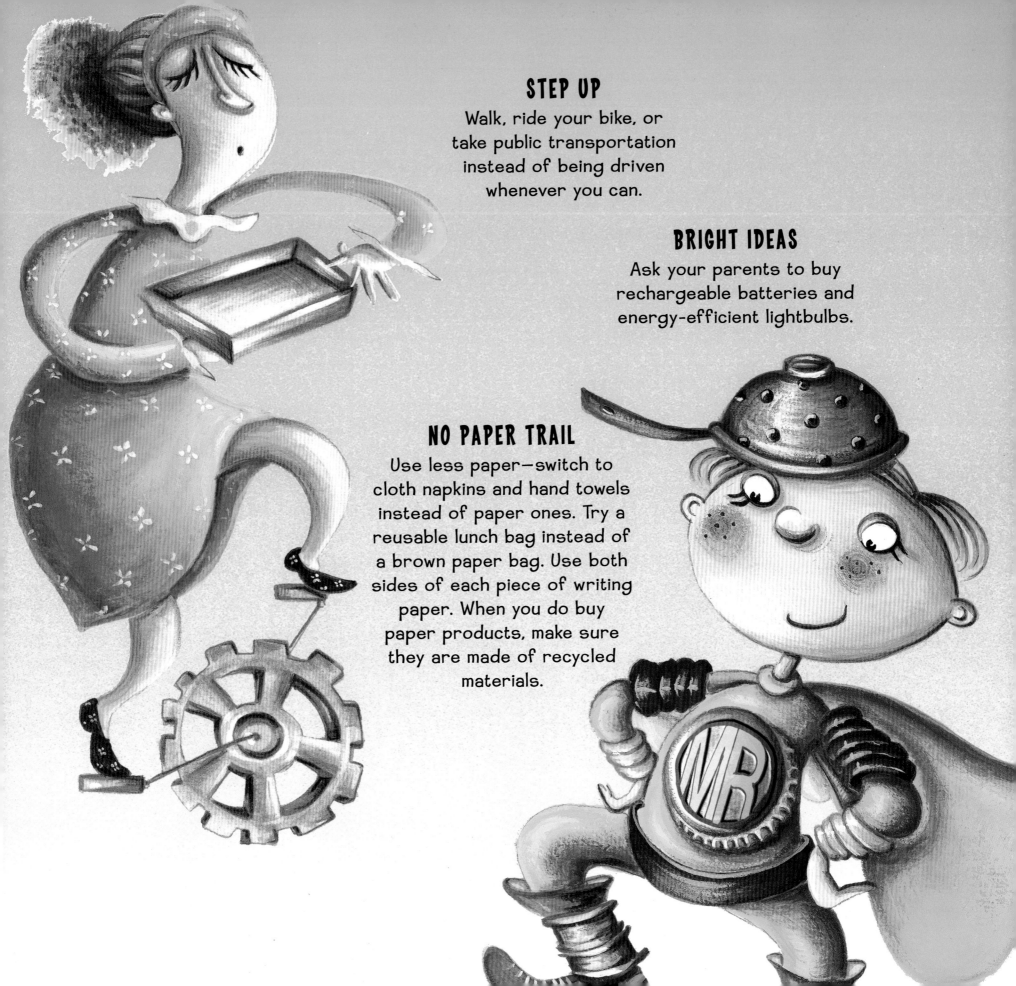

STEP UP

Walk, ride your bike, or take public transportation instead of being driven whenever you can.

BRIGHT IDEAS

Ask your parents to buy rechargeable batteries and energy-efficient lightbulbs.

NO PAPER TRAIL

Use less paper—switch to cloth napkins and hand towels instead of paper ones. Try a reusable lunch bag instead of a brown paper bag. Use both sides of each piece of writing paper. When you do buy paper products, make sure they are made of recycled materials.

The End